This book is
your passport
into time.

Can you survive
the American
Revolution?
Turn the page
to find out.

Bantam Books in the Time Machine Series
Ask your bookseller for the books you have missed

TIME █ MACHINE® 10

American Revolutionary

by **Arthur Byron Cover**
illustrated by **Walter Martishius**
and **Alex Nino**

A Byron Preiss Book

BANTAM BOOKS
TORONTO · NEW YORK · LONDON · SYDNEY · AUCKLAND

To Those Who Were There

RL 5, IL age 10 and up

AMERICAN REVOLUTIONARY
A Bantam Book/December 1985

Special thanks to Judy Gitenstein, Ann Hodgman, Anne Greenberg, Robin
Stevenson, Martha Cameron, Debbie Trentalange and Rosa Domenech.

Book design by Alex Jay
Cover painting by Alex Nino
Cover design by Alex Jay
Mechanicals by Studio J
Typesetting by David Seham Associates
Editor: Ann Weil

"Time Machine" is a registered trademark of Byron Preiss Visual Publications,
Inc. Registered in U.S. Patent and Trademark Office.

ISBN 0-553-25300-X

Published simultaneously in the United States and Canada

*Bantam Books are published by Bantam Books, Inc. Its trademark, consisting of the
words "Bantam Books" and the portrayal of a rooster, is Registered in U.S. Patent
and Trademark Office and in other countries. Marca Registrada. Bantam Books,
Inc., 666 Fifth Avenue, New York, New York 10103.*

PRINTED IN THE UNITED STATES OF AMERICA

0 9 8 7 6 5 4 3 2 1

ATTENTION TIME TRAVELER!

This book is your time machine. Do not read it through from beginning to end. In a moment you will receive a mission, a special task that will take you to another time period. As you face the dangers of history, the Time Machine will often give you options of where to go or what to do.

This book also contains a Data Bank to tell you about the age you are going to visit. You can use this Data Bank to help you make your choices. Or you can take your chances without reading it. It is up to you to decide.

In the back of this book is a Data File. It contains hints to help you if you are not sure what choice to make. The following symbol appears next to any choices for which there is a hint in the Data File.

To complete your mission as quickly as possible, you may wish to use the Data Bank and the Data File together.

There is one correct end to this Time Machine mission. You must reach it or risk being stranded in time!

THE FOUR RULES OF TIME TRAVEL

As you begin your mission, you must observe the following rules. Time Travelers who do not follow these rules risk being stranded in time.

1.
You must not kill any person or animal.

2.
You must not try to change history. Do not leave anything from the future in the past.

3.
You must not take anybody when you jump in time. Avoid disappearing in a way that scares people or makes them suspicious.

4.
You must follow instructions given to you by the Time Machine. You must choose from the options given to you by the Time Machine.

YOUR MISSION

Your mission is to go back in time and discover the identity of the man who fired the first shot of the American revolution, and bring back his musket.

From 1775 to 1781, the thirteen colonies on the North American continent fought a war of independence from England, then the mightiest power in the world.

By the rude bridge that arched the flood,
Their flag to April's breeze unfurled,
Here once the embattled farmers stood,
And fired the shot heard round the world.

So begins Ralph Waldo Emerson's famous poem "Concord Hymn," sung at the dedication of the Battle Monument in 1837.

Even then, the identity of the man who fired the first shot of the war, beginning the Battle of Lexington and Concord, in April 1775, was a mystery.

Your mission won't be easy. You must not steal the musket! And none of your efforts to get the musket should change history—or you'll be stranded in time!

 To activate the Time Machine, turn the page.

**TIME TRAVEL ACTIVATED.
Stand by for Equipment.**

EQUIPMENT

You will be dressed in clothes suitable for the time period in which your adventure is set. You will also be equipped with a fife—a high-pitched flute—in order to serve the colonial army, if necessary, as a musician, and not as a foot soldier.

You will also have a small pouch in which to carry things. Select one of the following items to bring with you:

1. A box of raisins
2. A knife
3. A mirror

 To begin your mission now, turn to page 1.

 To learn more about the time to which you will be traveling, go on to the next page.

DATA BANK

TIMELINE

December 14, 1774—New Hampshire patriots led by Major John Sullivan sweep down on Fort William and Mary and make away with valuable stores of ammunition.

April 19, 1775—Fighting between rebels and British at Lexington and Concord. The revolutionary war begins.

May 10, 1775—Fort Ticonderoga captured by Americans.

June 17, 1775—Second Continental Congress appoints George Washington Commander in Chief of armed forces.

July 4, 1776—Congress adopts the Declaration of Independence, drafted by Thomas Jefferson.

August 26, 1776—The American "Charge of the Light Brigade" occurs during the Battle of Brooklyn, when Lord Stirling leads 200 Marylanders in a charge on British lines.

September 11, 1777—British general Howe and his forces enter Philadelphia, and Congress flees to New York.

October 4, 1777—Washington withdraws from the field of battle and his forces retreat to Valley Forge.

May 4, 1778—Congress signs a treaty of alliance with France.

June 27, 1778—General Washington fights the British forces to a draw at the Battle of Monmouth.

October 19, 1781—Washington defeats General Cornwallis at Yorktown, thus ending the fighting of the war.

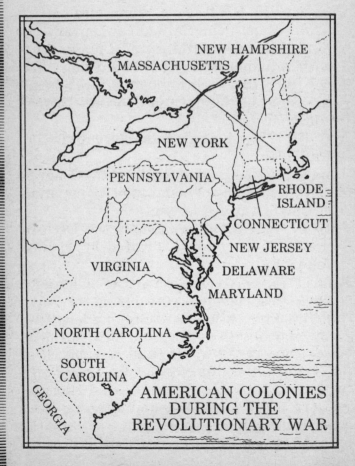

NEW HAMPSHIRE

MASSACHUSETTS

NEW YORK

PENNSYLVANIA

RHODE ISLAND

CONNECTICUT

NEW JERSEY

VIRGINIA

DELAWARE

MARYLAND

NORTH CAROLINA

SOUTH CAROLINA

GEORGIA

AMERICAN COLONIES DURING THE REVOLUTIONARY WAR

1) To a large degree, the revolutionary war began as a battle between the British Crown and the American colonies over taxes.

2) At the time of the revolutionary war, the well-trained British army was reputed to be the greatest in the world. The rebel army, on the other hand, was formed of hunters, farmers, and merchants.

3) Once the fighting began, the rebel forces had little idea what was expected of them as soldiers and as an army. After the Battle of Breed's Hill, on June 16, 1775, only the authority and willpower of General Israel Putnam succeeded in holding the rebel forces together.

4) At first the rebel troops were unwilling to be commanded by men from colonies different than their own, who were often appointed to posts according to their social prestige rather than their military skills.

5) General Washington managed to hold the forces together—and keep the cause of freedom alive—despite a cantankerous Congress, poor supplies, squabbling officers, and an ever-present toothache.

6) Because the British Empire then extended around the world, its commanders often hired mercenaries—paid soldiers from other countries—to beef up local forces. The British commanders in the colonies hired German soldiers called Hessians, and often enlisted American Indians as well.

7) The muskets of the era were flintlocks.

They were loaded through the muzzle and had, on the average, an accuracy of 80 to 100 yards.

8) Paul Revere, long a rider for Boston's rebel Committee of Safety, made his most famous ride on April 18, 1775, when he read a signal from the Old North Church: there would be one lamp in the tower if the British came by land, and two if by sea.

9) On August 27, 1776, George Washington's army, overwhelmed by superior forces, made a retreat from the Battle of Brooklyn. A brave attack by 200 Marylanders, led by Lord Stirling, prevented the British forces from winning a major victory.

10) Benedict Arnold was a prestigious American patriot who was respected, though not universally liked, before he became a traitor. He believed conquering Canada would lead to the end of the war—and a rebel victory. On October 11, 1776, Arnold's hastily assembled fleet was defeated by the British in a two-day battle near Valcour Island, in Lake Champlain.

11) British uniforms were red; hence the name *redcoats*. Rebel uniforms—when the rebels had them—were blue.

12) On May 4, 1778, Congress ratified the French-American alliance, changing the conflict from a civil war into a global war. Not only did France openly aid the colonies with supplies and men, but the British were forced to divert troops to their other holdings around

the world, thereby diluting their strength in the colonies.

13) The turning point of the war was the Battle of Monmouth, New Jersey, fought on June 27, 1778. Though the fight was really a draw, both sides claimed victory. However, the major forces in the north never again met in a major battle, and the rebel army eventually wore the British down.

14) A heroine of the Battle of Monmouth was a soldier's wife named Mary Ludwig Hayes, better known as Molly Pitcher. She loaded artillery during the battle and afterward nursed wounded soldiers.

15) One of General Washington's best officers was a young Frenchman, the Marquis de Lafayette, who preferred above all else to be in the thick of battle.

DATA BANK COMPLETED. TURN THE PAGE TO BEGIN YOUR MISSION.

 Don't forget, when you see this symbol, you can check the Data File in the back of the book for a hint.

ou are standing beside a New England country road. It is night, and the sweet odor of spring hangs in the cool air. An owl hoots, and the crickets chirp peacefully.

You wonder if the American Revolution has begun.

A quick look up and down the road shows it is deserted. There's no telling which way the nearest town lies, or even what time of night it is.

You pick the southerly direction and start walking. Soon the woods begin to thin, and the fields show signs of having been recently tended.

At least the road is covered with tracks—sure signs that it is frequently traveled, you think to yourself. You're making progress toward a town.

The cricket sounds suddenly cease. All you hear is the noise of your boots crunching against the road.

Wait!

You stop to listen.

Everything is silent. Unnaturally so.

What's that?

The clatter of horses' hooves in the distance, beyond the bend.

Suddenly the horses are drowned out by the louder approach of a single rider behind you!

You've no way of knowing who's who. Better play it safe and get out of sight—immediately!

You scramble up a tree. You're almost concealed in the branches when the single horseman nears the tree. You twist around to get a better look at him.

Wood snaps. Suddenly you get a sinking feeling, and it isn't just your stomach. The air whistles in your ears as you fall from the breaking branch.

You brace yourself for a hard landing, but hit a cushion before you'd expected to hit anything.

The cushion is the horse's rump. The rider falls with you as the horse continues running down the road.

"What's the meaning of this?" demands the rider, grabbing you and pulling you to your feet before you can recover. He looks very angry.

"Wait! I can explain! It's not what you think!"

He sneers, pulls you closer, and then his eyes widen in surprise. "You! I never expected betrayal from you!"

"What are you talking about? I don't even *know* you!"

"Yes, you do!" he insists, pushing you away in disgust. "Don't lie to me!"

"I swear, I've never seen you—!"

He takes off his hat to give you a better look at his face in the moonlight.

Vaguely aware of the approaching hoof-beats, you squint and lean forward. Come to think of it, there *is* something familiar about him. Those big hands, that large, squarish face . . .

Then it hits you. "You're Paul Revere!" With a little bit of luck, you've encountered him during his famous ride on the eve of the Battle of Lexington and Concord. The first shot of the Revolution will be fired soon.

"And you, my friend," Revere replies, "are no patriot!" The hoofbeats become so loud that even his all-consuming anger can no longer distract him. "The British are coming!" he exclaims, his attitude toward you suddenly changing for the better. "You were trying to warn me . . ."

"Not exactly," you say, as the British patrol, leading Revere's horse, comes round the bend.

The British lieutenant glowers at you for a moment, but when his eyes go to Revere, his expression hardens. He asks coldly, "Sir, may I crave your name?"

Feigning dizziness, you stagger to the lieutenant's horse and grab the bridle. You deliver a sloppy salute, pretend to nearly fall, and say, deliberately slurring your words, "It's nothing, officer; just a disagreement over who owns that horse. It's nothing we can't work out on our own."

"Silence!" snaps a sergeant, slapping you on the shoulder with his whip. You back away, out of his reach.

Ignoring you, the lieutenant repeats his question to Revere.

"My name is Paul Revere," he says boldly.

Three of the patrol immediately dismount and seize him. Revere does not resist, though he does appear concerned.

"Don't worry," says the lieutenant, leaning forward on his horse. "No harm shall come to you."

"However much you deserve it," growls one of the other British holding him.

"And however little good it will do you," Revere replies. "I've alarmed the countryside from here to Boston. Your British boats have been run aground, and by the time your delayed troops reach Lexington, five hundred men will fall upon them."

That doesn't sound right! The Old North Church in Boston should have signaled Revere with two burning lamps—indicating the British army was approaching by water, with the intention of seizing rebel supplies in Providence. The troops were never delayed.

Of course! He's told them a lie, in order to confuse *them*. The ploy seems to have worked.

"Silence!" barks the lieutenant at his men, who have been muttering among themselves. They stop talking immediately, with the discipline of well-trained dogs. They watch their superior intently as he dismounts, walks over to Revere, and sternly looks him in the eye. "You, sir," says the lieutenant, "are in a damned critical situation."

"I am sensible of it," Revere replies.

"And this one," says the lieutenant, pointing at you with his thumb, "must be one of your fellow rebel messengers."

Revere shrugs. "I don't know, sir. I must confess, I've never seen this person before in my life."

The lieutenant sneers, but before he can reply, a musket shot echoes through the countryside. So sudden and unexpected is the sound that the soldiers have a tough time keeping their horses from bolting, and the three men holding Revere are forced to release him to help their companions.

"What was that?" demands the lieutenant.

"To alarm the countryside, of course," says Revere, smiling broadly. "My compatriots are ready for the likes of you."

"Shall we execute him, sir?" asks a soldier eagerly.

"Or bring him to Lexington for a hanging?" inquires another.

The lieutenant considers the matter, then, shaking his head, walks to his horse. "No, we can't be bothered with prisoners," he says as he mounts. "And we've no bullets to waste on the likes of them." He looks at you and Revere in disgust. "Prepare to move out!" he barks at his men.

The patrol lines up in formation. The man in the rear holds the reins of Revere's horse.

The lieutenant turns to you and Revere. "Neither of you will ever ride *this* horse again!"

The patrol disappears around the bend, and the sound of hoofbeats recedes into the distance.

Revere slams his fist into his palm. "The irony of it! That gallant little horse has borne me and my news to every village in the countryside! Now he belongs to the British cavalry, and he'll do their business!"

"At least we're free to walk," you say, though you're not looking forward to the experience.

Revere puts his hand on your shoulder. "Again, I must thank you for having provided me with timely assistance."

"Anytime," you say, wondering what he means by "again."

Revere points across a field. "That way, if

I've my directions right, lies the farm of a friend, the good Reverend Jonas Clark. I'll go there and join my militia in the morning. You are welcome to accompany me."

Revere doesn't realize he's offering you the chance to take a walk with one of the most famous men in American history. It's tempting; maybe you should take him up on the offer. He might explain why he recognized you.

Or perhaps you should excuse yourself and jump directly to the Lexington-Concord battle.

You had better decide quickly. Revere's anxious to be off, and he's impatiently awaiting your reply.

 Stay with Revere. Turn to page 12.

 Jump ahead in time. Turn to page 15.

You are in pitch-blackness. The floor sways beneath you, and the gurgling water reeks of salt. You must be on a ship, but where? You feel around, looking for a way out. The wood floor is all coarse; you stop moving for a moment to pull several splinters from your hands.

What's that? Voices? You listen closely as the ship rolls back and forth.

You hear men speaking in excited, furtive whispers as they come aboard. Metal hinges creak, and just as a beam of moonlight shines in, you huddle in a corner.

An Indian peers in. An Indian raid at sea? Something peculiar's going on here.

"There be the goods, Jeremy!" says the Indian.

Another peers inside. "All that tasty tea. A shame to waste it all," he says, laughing.

Now you're sure something strange is going on. He doesn't sound at all like an Indian.

Suddenly you know where you are and when. You've landed smack in the middle of the Boston Tea Party of December 16, 1773.

Something tells you party crashers won't be welcome here tonight. You're about to jump when a hand falls heavily onto your shoulder. "Who be ye and what be ye doing here?" he demands.

"I . . . uh . . . was thinking of stowing away."

"Ye were not," he replies, leering.

"Ah . . . enlisting?"

The second explanation proves no better than the first. The disguised Bostonians pass you from man to man, head over head, toward the waiting ocean.

"We'll see if ye swim better than ye spy," says the last as he heaves you overboard.

You hear their laughter as you hit the water. You let yourself sink out of sight, below the surface.

Time to get back on the right track.

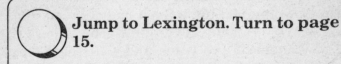
Jump to Lexington. Turn to page 15.

ou and Paul Revere briskly walk the two miles to the Reverend Jonas Clark's house. Revere is grim and silent during the journey. He must be wondering what will become of himself and his countrymen in the days ahead.

His mood lightens considerably, however, once he gets inside the Reverend Clark's house and sees John Adams and John Hancock inside. "You're safe!" he exclaims. "I was certain the redcoats would capture you."

"They came and asked for us," says Hancock, "and in fact they would have searched the house." He nods in the direction of a matronly woman taking a fresh loaf of bread from the stove. "But the reverend's good wife here threw them off the track and sent them on a wild-goose chase."

"A chase which eventually brought them to us," says Revere.

"Us?" asks Adams suspiciously. "Who's your friend here?"

"Yes, an excellent idea," you say, "as I must be off before dawn."

She gives you a few biscuits for your journey, and you say good night to everyone. Then you walk to the barn as if you actually intend to sleep there.

You throw down the blanket on a haystack, look around to make certain that no one is watching, and jump.

 Turn to page 21.

You smell the apple blossoms in the air. It must be spring, you think, as you watch the dawn lighten this roadside orchard.

In the field across the road, the king's redcoats are outmaneuvering the Lexington militiamen. The heavily outnumbered rebels will soon be at a further disadvantage: they're about to face the rising sun, and it will be much more difficult for them to see the redcoats clearly.

You scurry under a fence, run across the road, and drop into tall grass to wait and watch.

More rebels arrive at the edge of the wood. Popping out behind one tree and ducking behind another, each is visible for only an instant. Some reach the field and begin crawling forward on their bellies. Finally, they begin to stand and form ragged lines, to match those of the British on the other side of the field.

Almost fifty yards away, a youth with blond hair and a sharp, hawklike nose raises his flintlock rifle and aims at the British. The redcoats can't see him because he's hidden behind thick brush, but soon they'll know he's there, that's a certainty.

Wait! The youth is hesitating. His arms tremble. The panache of turkey feathers on the butt of his flintlock shakes as if blown about by a brisk breeze, though the air is hushed and still.

Another militiaman, hiding nearby, sees the lad, realizes what he is about to do, and whispers, "What rashness is this? Wait for the order to fire, lad, wait for orders!"

The youth lowers his flintlock with a start. "I'm sorry," he whispers back. "I was so scared I didn't realize what I was doing."

The wind carries their voices to your ears. A few other rebels look toward the pair and urge them to be quiet. You can feel the tension between the rebels and the redcoats. It's obvious that neither side wants to be the first to fire. But tempers are hot right now. They've been whittled to a cutting edge.

Anything can happen.

Then you hear the rising sounds of marching drums, the pounding of hoofbeats, and the relentless *stomp-clomp-stomp* of approaching infantrymen. You recognize British major Pitcairn leading his troops down a hill.

Pitcairn barks orders to someone, who in turn barks more orders to the troops. You don't understand what the people are saying, but

the resulting troop movement, closing in around the rebels, makes their intent quite plain.

The Americans try to disperse, but the British outflank them. They're outflanking you, too. The shooting's about to begin, and you're in the thick of it! You'd better move—fast!

You crawl through the grass toward the youth with the panache of turkey feathers on his flintlock. But you're not moving fast enough. You run with your back and knees bent.

"You ain't got no musket," someone growls behind you. "Get out of here before you get shot!"

"I'll be all right," you say, looking behind you just in time to trip over a log and fall, face-first, into a tall bush.

The bush shakes—violently—with the force of your landing.

You realize, with a sinking feeling in your stomach, that this unexpected motion on the field is not going to be well received by either side. And, as if to confirm the thought, the youth with the hawklike nose shouts *"Yeow!"* His trigger finger slips.

The sound of musket fire seems to echo to the horizon and back.

"You scared the dickens out of me!" exclaims the youth. Just then, twenty or thirty similar explosions fill the air.

"Great," you say aloud, covering your head as the musket balls whistle, "I'm responsible for the start of the revolutionary war."

But the youth doesn't seem to mind. He calmly reloads his musket, although the bush he's hiding behind isn't exactly solid cover. "No, you aren't," he says conversationally.

You take a good look at his features, memorizing them. This is the person you've come to find. And that musket—with the distinctive panache of turkey feathers—is the object you must win.

"Don't you know what's happening today?" you exclaim. "This is war!"

He grins. The situation amuses him. "This ain't war. This is just a little shootin'. I was gonna shoot anyway. That's why I came here in the first place."

Terrific! you think to yourself. You can't help but notice that the redcoats are continuing to fire, while the rebels are retreating into the woods—probably heading toward Concord.

"Let's get out of here," the kid says.

"Before we're the only ones left, uh, standing," you observe—to yourself, as it turns out. The kid has already taken off; he's a blur darting into the woods.

In fact, he's running like a greased rabbit. You'll never catch him now. It's too bad. You've got to get that musket!

You've no choice but to run, too, and listen to the whistle of passing musket balls. An especially shrill sound—like that of a rabid wasp—passes uncomfortably close to your ear.

By the time you reach the relative safety of the woods, the kid is nowhere to be seen. And British soldiers are moving into the woods to take potshots at stragglers like you.

You won't be able to find the youth now. But he'll probably be at another battle site in the near future.

You can jump ahead to Concord and try to meet up with him there. Or maybe you should jump ahead a few months to the next major battle site of the war: Fort Ticonderoga.

 Jump to Fort Ticonderoga. Turn to page 24.

 Jump to the Battle of Concord. Turn to page 36.

You are up to your knees in water. Fortunately the pond you're in isn't too deep, and it has a soft, muddy bottom.

Since you're already wet, there's no point in moving out of the shallow water until you have your bearings. The clear night sky is studded with stars.

Wait! What's that?

Someone's making noise in the distance. You peek through some bushes and see a man trying to uproot a small tree. He's grunting loudly. Two other men laugh and offer him encouragement, but they're not helping him.

You crawl out of the pond toward the men. Soon you're near enough to make out what they're saying.

"There! That ought to make old Putnam happy!" says the burly man as he finally succeeds in uprooting the tree.

"Now all you have to do is drag it back to the fort," says an older man, his arms loaded with firewood.

"But that's two miles away!" exclaims the burly man.

"You should have thought of that," says the youth. His arms are also loaded with firewood. "Still, Putnam'll be proud when you finally arrive at camp—two, three days hence."

You crawl closer, to get a better look at them.

"Say, I've an idea," the youth says. "Why don't we just go home?"

"Desert?" asks the burly man, searching for a good grip on the tree. He quickly settles on the tip of the branches.

"It's not as if we've enlisted," replies the youth.

"Perhaps not, Dan," says the older man, "but General Putnam has ordered us to stay together for the time being. It's his right as militia commander."

"Like it or not," says the burly man, "after the way we shot up the redcoats today on Breed's Hill, we're in this war for the duration."

"Good. Then tell me this, Louis, why can't we fight instead of gather wood?" asks the young Dan.

"Because icicles can't run," says the older man, answering for Louis.

You stand up. "Excuse me!"

Dan screams, drops his wood, and runs headlong into the forest, making more noise than you ever thought a single person could possibly make. He trips and falls, face-first, into the mud. You bite your lip to keep from laughing out loud.

"What's so funny?" asks the older man cold-ly. The burly one called Louis just stares at you. And young Dan, his face covered with mud, glares at you.

"Uh, nothing's funny," you say meekly. "I didn't mean to scare him. I was just passing through."

"Do you know this person?" the older one asks Louis.

"Certainly not," says Louis.

They ask you your name, and you tell them.

"Never heard of you," says the older man. "Or of your family." He drops his wood and hefts his knife. "I'm betting you're a spy."

Louis advances. "Time to answer a few questions. Maybe your last questions, redcoat."

No, it's time to turn and run. And you do. Twigs and branches scratch your body and face. You may be able to outrun these guys, but just doing that isn't going to help you accomplish your mission.

It's time to jump to the battle at Lexington. But which way? Do you jump back in time? Or into the future?

Better decide—quickly!

Jump to the past. Turn to page 15.

Jump to the future. Turn to page 28.

The stars glow overhead like a thousand infernos. You're on a cliff overlooking the gate of Fort Ticonderoga.

The moonlight makes the landscape and the fort below shimmer like a dreamland. A single guard naps, standing up, against the gate inside the walls.

And now that your ears, as well as your eyes, have adjusted to the forest and the night, you hear the redcoats snoring peacefully inside the barrack houses.

Isn't anybody on guard here? you wonder.

But then again, why should they be alert? This fort is situated exactly in the middle of nowhere.

What's that? You glimpse a silent, furtive movement in the forest.

There! Another!

And another!

Like shadows, rebels move out of the forest. They're all wearing buckskins, except for one,

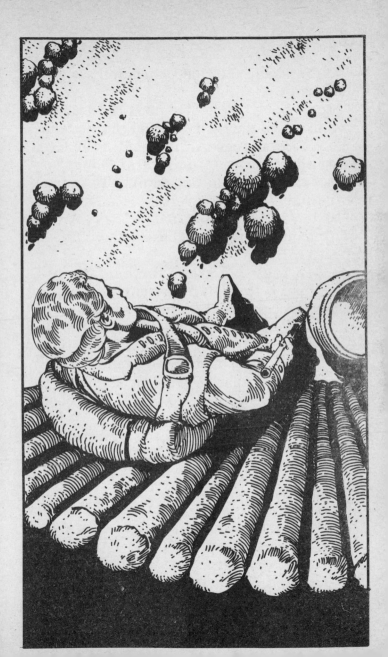

who's dressed in the blue-coated uniform of the rebel army.

"Stand back, Arnold!" snaps the leader to the man in uniform. "I demand the surrender of Fort Ticonderoga in the name of the Great Jehovah and the Continental Congress." Then, to the men in buckskins: "Fire at my command!"

"Listen to me, Ethan Allen!" says Arnold. "I'm in command here! These men will fire at my say-so!"

Before they can argue further, you hiss, "Hey! Listen to me! There's only one man at the gate! I can take him out for you!"

Ethan Allen and Benedict Arnold look around, evidently unable to see you in the tree. You pick up a rock and drop it. *Whack!* It lands on the guard's head. He slumps to the ground, groans and passes out. He'll probably awaken with a splitting headache.

"Get some men to climb the wall!" you tell Allen and Arnold. "They'll open the gates and you'll be able to capture the British without firing a shot."

That's exactly what happens. By the time you climb down the cliff and enter the fort, Ethan Allen's Green Mountain Boys—as his men call themselves—have awakened the redcoats and put them in the guardhouse.

"I don't know where you came from," Allen says, shaking your hand, "but you certainly saved us a lot of trouble."

"Glad to do it," you say sheepishly.

Arnold appraises you in a suspicious way you don't like. "I think you might be a spy. It's entirely possible, Mr. Allen, that your woodsmen tipped off these regiments. The commander of this fort saw that resistance would be futile. He decided to make sure you got credit for this victory—instead of me!"

"Your men are still twenty leagues away, Arnold," replies Allen. "Remember?"

"That has nothing to do with it. I think this person is a spy and should be held for questioning. *My* men will do the job."

Well, well. It looks as if Benedict Arnold has some unpleasant things in mind for you. Not very nice for a man who eventually turned against his country.

Maybe you can turn the tables on Arnold, by denouncing him as a traitor before he can do the same to you. Or you can just try to answer his questions right now.

Allen and Arnold are both staring at you thoughtfully, waiting for your response.

 Denounce Arnold. Turn to page 32.

 Cooperate with questioning. Turn to page 30.

ou're in a gulley, at night. Not ten yards away, up the hill, walks a redcoat patrol. So this is what it feels like to be hunted.

You scoot backward, accidentally rustling a bush.

"What was that?" a redcoat exclaims.

Then the patrol is completely silent. You do not move, trying to hold your breath.

"A pox on these colonists!" says another redcoat when his patience has run out. "I've never before encountered such a stubborn folk!"

"The colonists have always been stubborn," says the first redcoat. "That's why their ancestors came here in the first place."

"Sshh!" says a third. "Maybe we can scare some sense into this one."

They approach, poking their bayonets among the bushes and the foliage. It's pitch-black in the woods. The farther they get from the fourth man holding the torch on the trail, the more difficult it becomes for them to see.

You can barely see the redcoats. If you move, they will certainly hear you.

One of the redcoats, you see by his silhouette, is getting uncomfortably close. He jabs his bayonet savagely in your general vicinity. He's bound to trip over you, if he doesn't poke you first.

 Time to jump, before he finds you! Turn to page 9.

came to the fort to see a friend of mine," you explain to Allen and Arnold. "I heard he might have been assigned to Captain Arnold's expedition."

"Why must you see him?" asks Allen.

"To give him a message—of a rather personal nature. It's from . . . oh . . . his mother," you say as two Green Mountain Boys help you stand.

"Your tale's nonsense," Arnold sneers. "Since I'd already left civilization before you accepted your assignment, I'd like to know just how you managed to arrive here before me."

"I, uh, took a few shortcuts."

Allen slaps you hard on the back, so hard you almost fall down again. "Hah? See the truth of the matter? I'd wager our friend here knows the countryside better than any of your mapmakers, Captain."

"One more thing," says Arnold, ignoring Allen's insolence. "Why were you up yonder tree?"

"To have a better view of the action," you reply. "How was I to know I would fall?"

Suddenly, much to your surprise, Arnold throws back his head and laughs uproariously. There's no malice in his voice. Evidently you've convinced him. "Then stay, my friend," he says, "and seek out your man—when my forces arrive two days hence."

Two days! That's a lot of time.

Still, you've got to make a decision, one way or the other. Do you wait to see if the youth from the battle at Lexington arrives with the rest of the forces in a few days, or do you back-track to Concord, the day after the shooting at Lexington?

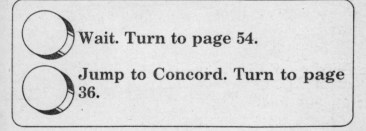

Wait. Turn to page 54.

Jump to Concord. Turn to page 36.

don't have to answer the questions of a man who's as big a traitor as this country's ever seen, sir!" you say to Benedict Arnold.

You have just enough time to see Allen smile to himself before something hits you on the back of the head and you black out.

You wake up in the guardhouse, which is a bare room with a dirt floor. A blanket is wadded up in the corner. One of the soldiers is standing guard over you.

"How can Ethan Allen do this to me after I helped you folks capture the fort?" you ask the guard.

"You did nothing we couldn't have done for ourselves," replies the guard. "As for Mr. Allen, he doesn't have to like this Arnold to respect him as a fellow freedom fighter. Otherwise, he would have shot the popinjay long ago."

It seems you've come to a dead end here. You curl up in the blanket and pretend to sleep. Soon the guard leans against the wall outside your cell and snores peacefully.

Jump to Concord. Turn to page 36.

You are in the midst of
the New Jersey wilderness, near the banks of
a mighty river.

Soon you hear soldiers with British accents
laugh drunkenly from somewhere near you in
the forest. One says, "What was that, mate?"

"Don't know," says another. "Should we
take a look around?"

"Naw," says the third. "Here. Have another
drink."

Their voices tell you approximately where
they are. The moon provides you with enough
light to move fairly easily through the brush.
You sneak forward cautiously, not daring to
rustle a leaf.

Suddenly a musket shot rings out. You dive
to the ground for cover as the shot echoes
through the woods.

"What did you do that for?" asks a redcoat.

"Just to hear what a rebel's musket sounds
like when he's not hiding behind a tree."

Now that's an unfair accusation, you observe, carefully parting the branches of a bush
so you can get a better view of the three redcoat stragglers sitting around the fire.

Josh, his hands tied behind his back, sits on

a log. The redcoat casually tosses the smoking musket on the ground so he can take the bottle being offered by his rotund companion.

"Careful with that hardware," Josh snaps. "That musket was a gift from my uncle. It has a long and proud history . . ."

"Of killing Englishmen!" yells a short redcoat indignantly.

"We didn't ask for this war!" says Josh. "We only wanted our rights!"

The redcoats shout him down immediately, and soon all four men are arguing loudly among themselves.

Listening to them, you learn that the redcoats hope to catch up with the main body of their army tomorrow. They figure that with a prisoner in their hands, their superiors won't ask too many questions about what they were doing so far behind.

You must rescue Josh! You think you can wait for the redcoats to settle down, then sneak behind Josh and cut his bonds with your Swiss army knife. Then you can retrieve his musket before you escape.

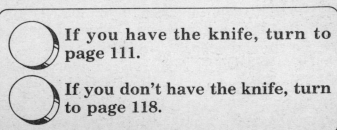

If you have the knife, turn to page 111.

If you don't have the knife, turn to page 118.

You're behind a stone wall, near the British line of retreat at the Battle of Concord. Just as you're about to peek over the wall, a musket ball careens off its top, spraying the area with pebbles.

You decide to crawl to the end and look around instead.

A troop of redcoats, strung out over half a mile, makes its way down the road. Rebels fire upon it from either side, yet the redcoats don't falter or run. The rebels are making good use of the natural and man-made camouflage, while the redcoats stand in plain sight and try to fire back.

The redcoats aren't used to this sort of fight, you realize. This isn't the organized kind of battle they've been trained for.

Stray musket balls are flying everywhere. You see a sign across the road: Hartwell's Tavern. You hope it'll be a good place to find some cover. You dart across the road, climb the gate, run up the steps, and knock on the door. Hard.

"Let me in!" you yell into the door. "Let me in! Please!"

"Are you a Tory—or a Whig?" asks a man behind the door.

"Neither! I just don't want to get shot!"

The door opens, and a grizzled tavernkeeper with sharp eyes pulls you in by the collar. "Take that musket by the window there," he orders, "and stand ready."

The last thing you want to do is hurt somebody. You'll just have to fake it.

You reach the window just in time to see a redcoat dash up the steps and knock on the door. The tavernkeeper looks down at his trigger finger, and his forehead breaks into a sweat. But he doesn't pull the trigger.

"Open the door in the name of the king!" shouts the redcoat.

"Why should I?" replies the tavernkeeper. Gathering his courage, he leans out a window and takes a wild shot at the redcoat, who responds by dashing to the side of the house.

Several other redcoats, you notice, have stopped in front of the tavern. The men converse in whispers, and some occasionally nod in your direction.

"What are they going to do?" you ask.

"There's no telling. They look awful angry,

if you ask me. Go upstairs, won't you, and see how my wife and children are doing."

You run up the stairs into the hall. At the other end is an open door. Inside you see only a corner of the bed, but you can hear two frightened children crying. Their mother is trying to soothe them.

Right now, no one can see you. You can jump out of this mess to some time when the fighting's died down.

Or you can stay here and help these people.

Better decide quickly before you lose your chance.

 Stay here. Turn to page 43.

 Jump in time. Turn to page 48.

ou're sitting up to your stomach in the waters of a marsh, surrounded on all sides by redcoats during the American "Charge of the Light Brigade." The flamboyant officer, Lord Stirling, is leading what's left of two hundred cavalrymen against an onslaught of British infantrymen and artillery fire, in an effort to break through their lines during the Battle of Brooklyn.

The musket? Where is it? you wonder, though the answer is obvious: the musket is exactly where it should be. You're going to have to devise an *honest* way of gaining possession of it.

You see three redcoats taking aim at Lord Stirling. You run up to them and push over the nearest one, knocking all three down like a row of bowling pins.

One of them kicks your legs out from under you before you can get away. You fall face-first into the marsh. You wipe the mud from your eyes to see three redcoat bayonets pointing at you.

"Let's take care of this one fast!" a redcoat growls.

"Help!" you yell, hoping you won't have to jump while these men can see you.

Lord Stirling has heard your call. He turns his horse around and rides toward you and the three redcoats at a full gallop. "No!" he shouts. "That youngster saved my life and shall not fall today!"

Lord Stirling's horse slams into two of the men, sending them flying. The third man runs away for a few yards, then stands his ground and readies to shoot.

But Lord Stirling twists his horse around and slams it into him, too.

It's time to get away from here, you think as you scramble away. But Lord Stirling's horse trips and falls, and he is thrown out of the saddle. He lands on a dry patch of ground with a tremendous *thunk!*

You rush to his side. He seems stunned, but otherwise all right.

"Come on! We've got to get out of here!" you urge, helping him to stand.

But it's already too late. The two of you have been captured by a veritable regiment of redcoats.

"Aha! We've got us an officer!" says one of the men.

You and Lord Stirling have no choice but to surrender and hope to escape another time.

 Turn to page 78.

ou run down the hall and into the children's room. Their mother is huddled beneath the blanket with the children, hiding.

"Have mercy on me!" she cries.

"Don't worry," you say. "I'm on your side."

You hear shots outside and rush to the window. The stable grounds are swarming with angry redcoats. "There's no time to talk now," you say. "We've got to get you out of here!"

"Let's go out the back door," says the woman. "Follow me."

Shots explode downstairs. The four of you reach the back door just as a redcoat kicks it open in your face!

You go flying hard against the wall. Your breath is slammed from your lungs. You have a tough time getting it back. Things get hazy and start going around in circles. You're vaguely aware of the children darting into another room. The redcoat positions his bayonet above your stomach.

The woman steps between you and the redcoat. "No!" she cries. "Have mercy!"

The redcoat's mouth twitches, and his face pales. "You're both traitors," he says between clenched teeth. "How dare you rise up against the king?" But the redcoat lowers his bayonet a few inches. A few more, and you might be safe. . . .

A shot rings out. The redcoat's eyes go wide. He spins around, raises his bayonet again, and promptly falls dead to the floor.

A portly rebel, nearing middle age, appears in the doorway, kneels, and inspects the corpse. "Gone to his reward," he says, not without some sadness.

"My husband!" the woman exclaims. She runs down the hall, followed by her children, who had been hiding in the linen closet.

The rebel picks up the corpse and unceremoniously heaves it out the back door. Then he turns to you. "What's your name, friend?"

You tell him, then ask his.

"I'm Benjamin Hogan, the printer."

Aha! During colonial times, printers wrote most of the newspapers they published, and they were among the most influential people in their communities. They knew practically everyone around.

"Say, maybe you can help me. I'm looking for a young fellow who did me a favor a few days ago, and then left before I had a chance to, ah, pay him back."

"Loaned you a few coins, eh?" Hogan says. "I'd be glad to help. Who is this person?"

"Well . . . I don't know his name."

"A challenge! I like that! What does he look like?"

You concentrate on that brief meeting and realize that in the heat of the moment, you were unable to memorize the youth's features.

You tell Hogan about his curly blond hair, hawklike nose, and buck teeth.

Hogan grimaces. "No. That doesn't sound like anyone I know. Not offhand, anyway."

"There was a panache on his musket—a batch of turkey feathers."

Hogn smiles. "Oh, that whippersnapper! He probably stole them from some Indian. Or from a relative who stole them from an Indian. Don't know who he is, but he was right next to me a little while ago. He's probably still chasing redcoats up the road a piece. If you hurry, you might catch him."

"Thanks! I think I will!" you say, taking off out the door.

You move up the road, past dead and wounded of both sides. The trees gradually thicken into another heavily wooded area, providing even more cover for the rebels. The British redcoats will stick out in these woods like sparklers on a clear summer night.

Several rebels up ahead have become bold enough to step out from behind their cover.

One of the rebels has a panache of feathers on his musket. The feathers are almost as bright as the redcoats' uniforms.

This must be your man!

He spots something—or someone—off a distance in the woods. He moves off the road, into the trees.

You follow. About a hundred yards from the road, the youth stops suddenly and stares in-

tently at a thick clump of bushes. He steps forward, bends down a little, and points his musket at the bush.

The bush shakes. He fires.

A wounded redcoat lunges from the bush and grabs for his throat. The youth jumps out of the way, and the redcoat collapses in a heap on the ground, dead.

The youth slowly lowers his musket. For several long moments he stares solemnly at the corpse, as if he expected it somehow to rise from the dead and finish its undone work.

Then he faints.

You look at him lying there, the musket by his side . . .

You look to the bridge, where the skirmish is winding down. No one seems to have noticed that the youth with the panache of turkey feathers on his musket is missing.

What should you do? You can wake the lad and try to make friends, so you can try to keep up with him throughout the course of the war.

Or you can try to cut this mission short and simply take the musket, bringing it back with you to the present.

 Help the rebel. Turn to page 51.

 Take the musket. Turn to page 39.

You are underwater—under *very cold* water. It freezes and chokes you at the same time. If you don't get some air quickly, you'll drown.

You kick up toward the surface. The more you kick, the faster you go. You just hope it's fast enough!

Pretty soon you see the surface rippling above you, as well as the underside of a canoe being rowed through the water.

You break through the surface. *Air!* It never felt so good before. You manage to take in a few gulps before a cannonball slams a direct hit on the canoe.

The water churns with the force of the hit. You duck below the surface and swim around until you reach some of the floating debris. You grab a plank of wood and use it to buoy yourself upwards. You pull yourself through the surface and try to get your bearings.

Other men hold onto other segments of the canoe.

In the distance looms a small fleet of British war vessels. Rebel canoes and boats are already fleeing from the barrage of cannon fire.

Where are you? you wonder, as you tread water.

Then you see the dapper figure of Benedict Arnold on one of the boats, cajoling his clumsy crew. You realize that you're near Valcour Island, witnessing the decimation of Arnold's ragtag American fleet.

Obviously you've made the wrong decision. If you're going to find the man who fired the first shot of the revolutionary war, you'll have to return to Concord.

But do you go to the past? Or to the future?

It's imperative that you decide quickly. The cannon fire is thick and fast, and very indiscriminate!

Jump back in time. Turn to page 36.

Jump forward in time. Turn to page 60.

ou kneel beside the inexperienced youth who fired the first shot at Lexington. It's difficult for you to believe he was the one who touched off a war that would last for seven years.

He's still out. You drag him behind some bushes. The fighting at the bridge seems to have moved on, but you're still relieved to be out of sight of the road.

You crawl to the slain redcoat, retrieve his canteen, and throw drops of water on the lad's face. His eyes blink. "Where am I?" he asks blankly, in a hoarse voice.

"Here. Drink some of this," you say, handing him the canteen.

He drinks deeply, nearly choking. "The redcoat—?" he asks between swigs. "What happened to him?"

You tell him.

The youth stares off into the forest. Something in his eyes indicates he isn't quite as inexperienced as he was during your first encounter. "You know, I'd been shooting at redcoats all day, and the longer it went on, the more surprised I got that the fighting hadn't stopped." He takes another swig. "What you'd said to me finally sank in. Maybe *this is war!* I suppose I followed the redcoat to find out if it really was. Now I know it is."

You put your hand on his shoulder. "Do you

want the fighting to stop?"

"I don't want to fight, but I have to." He touches his breast. "I feel it *here*. My countrymen and I won't live without our rights as Englishmen. We have the right to govern ourselves. Say, friend, what's your name?"

You tell him. "What's yours?"

"Shutesbury, Joshua E. Friends call me Josh," he says in a friendly tone. "We'd best be getting on our way."

"Where are you headed?" you ask.

"Guess I'll catch up to the main forces and do whatever it is most of the fellows are doing."

"How long do you intend to stay with them?"

"Till it's over, I suppose. Though I don't really know." He smiles and blushes. "My fiancée's pa has a farm outside Wellesley. He might need some help come harvesting time." Suddenly his eyes grow suspicious. "You're asking a lot of questions."

"Sorry. I didn't mean to," you stammer. "I guess I'm just naturally curious about the man who fired the first shot of the war."

Josh nods to himself. "I didn't fire the first shot of this, uh, war, I don't care what you say."

You're shocked, though you try to hide it. "Wh-what are you talking about?"

"My uncle fired the first shot—at Fort William and Mary. That was back in December of last year."

Could Emerson have been wrong when he wrote his famous poem?

"Well, that's interesting," you say, hoping you sound casual. "Who is your uncle?"

"His name's Randolph Shutesbury."

"Where is he these days?"

"The frontier. Somewhere in Pennsylvania. I don't know for certain."

You nod, and the two of you walk in silence the remainder of the way toward the road, which is strewn with the dead, unconscious, and wounded. It's not a pretty sight.

"Well, I've got some relatives down the road a piece," you say, heading back toward Hartwell's Tavern. "I'd better see if they're okay."

Josh waves good-bye, then trots across the bridge toward the rest of the rebel forces pursuing the British.

You watch him disappear around a bend. No one can see you now. This is a good time to jump.

You know you must find Josh's uncle Randolph. But should you try to find him in the Pennsylvania frontier? Or should you jump back in time to Fort William and Mary?

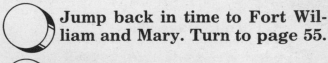

Jump back in time to Fort William and Mary. Turn to page 55.

Jump ahead in time to the frontier. Turn to page 62.

ou've decided to wait at Fort Ticonderoga for two days, to see if the blond youth arrives with Benedict Arnold's forces.

Actually, the wait is more like three days. You spend the time talking to the men and getting to know them, and watching rival commanders Benedict Arnold and Ethan Allen jostle for the credit of capturing the fort.

When the New England forces do arrive, the youth is not among them, nor can you find anyone who recognizes your description. It was a good try, but it's been a waste of time.

Better backtrack to the Battle of Concord.

Turn to page 36.

t's December 14, 1774. You're on a barren, snowcapped ridge overlooking a bare forest and some brush.

One of the bushes seems especially thick and full. It has a foot. The foot has a moccasin. The moccasin belongs to an Indian leaning forward from concealment, looking toward the path between the ridge and the forest.

The Indian has two friends looking with him.

You wonder if they noticed you as you crouch low behind a boulder. You're afraid to move. The ground is studded with gravel, and the slope is steep—a sure recipe for a smooth, noisy move.

You're afraid to breathe. You stifle a sneeze and wait. The Indians must be waiting for something, too. Or someone.

A bird sings. Rather loudly, you think. One of the Indians sings back. It's a signal! Whatever's going to happen, it won't be long now.

Sure enough, in a matter of moments the

sound of galloping hoofbeats echoes from the ridge, gradually becoming louder and louder.

The Indians hastily notch arrow to bow and prepare to fire on the approaching rider.

You pick up a rock and swing your arm back, ready to throw. But you hesitate. The rider may be an innocent man, but you can't act if it will change history.

The arrows fly. Two miss, but the third strikes the man through the shoulder. The man falls off the horse, but he keeps hold of the reins, bringing the animal down with him.

You catch a glimpse of the man's face. It's Paul Revere!

You throw the rock at the visible Indian and hit him on the arm. That Indian won't be shooting any more arrows today, anyway. But the other two, bow and arrow ready, rise up from the foliage and prepare to shoot at you!

Revere, still behind his horse, fires his musket at one. The Indian falls.

While the other turns around, momentarily wondering which person he should shoot at first—you or Revere—you rush down the slope. Its angle lets you work up a tremendous speed. You collide with the Indian and roll with him down the slope.

When you reach the bottom, the Indian is unconscious.

"Are you all right, Mr. Revere?" you ask.

The silversmith struggles to a standing position and then lets his horse up. "I'm fine," he says, though obviously he really isn't. His expression is set in a pained grimace. "You've the advantage of me. What's your name?"

You've met Revere before. Doesn't he remember you? Then it dawns on you—you met Revere in your past, but your first meeting with him lies in his future! You tell him your name, then ask: "Is there anything I can do to help?"

"Yes. Break off this arrow," he says, turning his back to you.

You're sickened by the prospect, but you do as he asks.

As Revere takes the canteen from his saddle and drinks deeply, you ask, "What do we do now? You need medical attention, and we should get away from these Indians. They'll wake soon."

"One of them won't," says Revere bitterly, handing you the canteen. "But don't worry about me. There are some settlers about a mile away who will help me. I can get there on my own."

"What about me?"

"Can you ride a horse?"

"Yes, I think so."

"Good. Right about now John Sullivan and his men should be, ah, seizing gunpowder and other supplies from the British at Fort William and Mary. I should know, because I was the one who gave Sullivan his orders from Adams and Hancock."

"Then what's the problem?"

"Well, I was on my way home when I passed that settlement I mentioned." Revere gasps for breath, takes the canteen, and drinks again. "A farmer there told me he had spotted a British squad on patrol on the way back to the fort. Someone has to warn Sullivan there might be a surprise attack."

"And that someone is me?"

"If you're a patriot, yes."

You know that Sullivan and his men succeeded in seizing the gunpowder, so you know that warning them won't change history. You also know that Revere will survive his wound to make his famous ride before the Lexington-Concord battle. So it looks as if you're going to be part of history again.

Despite his wound, Revere helps you climb into the saddle. "My country thanks thee," he says. "I pray that someday we shall meet again."

"I'm certain of it!" you say, as you begin your ride toward Fort William and Mary. If you hurry, you may make it there before the first shot is fired!

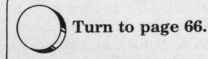

Turn to page 66.

You're in pitch blackness, a captive aboard the infamous British ship *New Jersey,* where thousands of rebel prisoners were held during the revolutionary war.

Crying and groaning, sick and starving men huddle together in the massive hold.

You'd jump from here in a hot second, but too many people would see you go. Perhaps it wouldn't matter anyway; most rebels brought to the *New Jersey* died of disease or starvation.

Still, you can't risk being stranded in time. Certainly not here.

There's only one thing to do, and that's play dead. You lie completely still, breathing as shallowly as possible.

You feel the men closest to you move away a few inches—which is as far as they can go. Your fellow prisoners must think you're dead. Now all you have to do is fool the British.

"Rebels! Show us your dead!" cries a voice from above.

"Here's one," croaks a prisoner near you.

You can't look around to see if he's pointing at you, or if the sailors coming down the steps have noticed. You can only stare straight ahead and hope your plan works.

It does.

"Strange," says one of the sailors carrying you up the stairs. "I've never seen a corpse on this ship look so healthy."

"Why don't you poke it with a stick to see if it fights back?" asks the other.

"Naw. It won't matter anyway."

Their words get you to thinking. What are they talking about? Just what do they do with their dead?

You find out when the sailors unceremoniously toss you overboard. There's no question what you should do now. You sink below the surface and jump back in time to Concord! You've come to a dead end in more ways than one.

Turn to page 36.

You are in the greenest, most beautiful forest you've ever seen, on a humid summer day. In the distance stand the majestic, weather-beaten Allegheny Mountains.

A group of cabins stands in a clearing between you and the mountains. This must be the settlement where Randolph Shutesbury lives. Walking toward the cabins, you marvel at all the work it must have taken to clear this land.

Something catches your eye. It looks like a bare man wearing only a loincloth, a headband and feathers. That can mean only one thing: *Indians!*

You run toward the settlement. As you get closer, you can make out the women feeding the barnyard animals and washing clothes in tubs of water. You shout out a warning, but they're too far away—or else too immersed in their work—to hear you.

You keep running as fast as you can. You're almost out of breath. You want to stop and rest for a minute, but several more Indians are crouching behind the forest's cover. You glimpse one notching his arrow to his bow. Another raises his war club. You can't stop now!

The Indian waits for you to run past him, then fires. You hear the arrow whistle through the air. It whizzes past you.

"Indians!" you yell to the women. "Indians! You're under attack!"

One of the women looks up just as Indian war whoops fill the air. Two more arrows whiz by you. The women jump up and run into the cabins. You hear the slamming of the wooden doors echoing from the mountains.

To your left is a patch of wood. You veer in that direction, pumping your legs as fast as you can. Your lungs hurt. It's getting harder and harder to breathe.

Just a few more yards . . .

You dive into a clump of bushes. Arrows fly through the foliage, but the twigs and branches deflect them from you. You're safer than you were a few moments ago, but you're pinned down. It's only a matter of time before an arrow finds its mark.

A musket fires. The sound of its explosion echoes throughout the valley.

The wave of arrows stops. There are two

more musket shots, and then there is . . . silence.

Is it all over?

You peek out of the bushes to see three frontiersmen, wearing buckskins, walk proudly through the clearing. They've fought off the Indians.

The big man in front has his musket slung over his shoulders.

You crawl out of the bushes and walk toward the men.

"I think I owe you one," says the burly man when he reaches you. "You warned my family. Though it was a lucky thing we got back from our hunting when we did—well, we might not have been so lucky."

You look into his eyes. "It was, uh, nothing."

He holds out his hand. "The name's Randolph Shutesbury. Pleased to make your acquaintance."

He stares at you strangely as he takes your hand. If he's met you before, he's going to recognize you. If not, it could make a big difference in how fast you accomplish your mission.

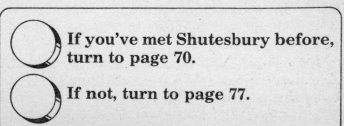

If you've met Shutesbury before, turn to page 70.

If not, turn to page 77.

You're riding like the wind on Paul Revere's horse, off to warn John Sullivan and his men about the possibility of a surprise British attack while they're capturing Fort William and Mary.

Navigating the narrow trail on the galloping horse demands your complete concentration. You lean over, close to the steed's neck. The cold air slaps your face. Your fingers are growing numb, but you don't dare loosen your grip on the reins even for a second.

You round a bend.

What's that ahead? Beyond the trees, spots of red are moving around, standing out in the white snow like giant cardinals. That can only mean you're getting close to the squad of redcoats.

Revere told you how to reach the fort, but you don't know the countryside well enough to try to go around them.

All right, you decide, I'll go through them.

You kick the horse. "Faster!" you urge.

The redcoats are marching boldly down the road. Beyond them is the fort, but it's too far away for you to make out anyone.

Wait! About fifty yards beyond the redcoats, between them and the fort, buckskinned rebels are hiding behind tree trunks, their muskets pointing at the opening gate.

Out steps a redcoat officer holding a white flag. You're just in time! Sullivan has convinced the soldiers inside to surrender.

So far the squad on patrol hasn't acted as if it's noticed anything amiss, and you're willing to bet Sullivan's men haven't noticed the redcoats. The situation is likely to change at any moment.

"Look out!" you yell, as your horse barrels you through the squad, scattering the men from the trail. "More redcoats! More redcoats!"

Some of the rebels turn to face you. A big burly man raises his musket and points it in your direction. The musket has a panache of turkey feathers on its stock.

What's going on? you wonder. Is he going to shoot at me?

The burly man fires the musket. The very air seems to explode with a loud *cra-ackk!*

Instinctively, you press down against the horse's neck. You can almost see the musket ball as it whizzes by.

A redcoat behind you cries out.

You sigh with relief, pulling the reins to slow down the horse.

"Surrender!" cries the burly man to the redcoat patrol. "We've already won the fort! Surrender!"

"It's true!" shouts the officer with the white flag. "Throw down your arms!"

The burly man grabs the bridle of the horse as it comes to a halt. You try to hide your surprise. The burly man fired the first shot of the day—you hope—but that panache is just like the one Josh had on his musket.

"That was a brave thing you did," says the burly man as he helps you off the horse. "By the way, my name's Randolph Shutesbury."

You introduce yourself and say, "That was a good shot. Thanks."

"You're welcome. I pride myself on my good shooting."

You and Randolph watch as two redcoats help the wounded man walk toward the fort.

"Looks as though he's going to be all right," you say.

"Good," says Randolph. "We captured that fort without firing a shot. All we want is the supplies. They might be handy for a day I hope never comes. I would have hated to have . . ." He trails off, not even wanting to say what might have happened to the soldier.

"That's quite a nice musket you have there," you say. "Mind if I take a look at it?"

"No. Here." Randolph hands it to you. "It's getting a little old, though. I'm thinking about getting a new one in Philadelphia before settling in the frontier with my family. I might give this to my nephew Josh."

Which is exactly what you will do, you observe to yourself. It's time to make your goodbyes and find Joshua Shutesbury at the next major campaign in which he takes part. Then you can find some way of gaining ownership of this musket.

Turn to page 73.

andolph Shutesbury's mood suddenly brightens. His eyes go wide and a big smile erupts across his face.

"I know you!" he exclaims, as he and his friends walk you toward the Pennsylvania frontier settlement. "You're the one I rescued from those soldiers at Fort William and Mary!"

"Is that the same musket?" you ask innocently, raising an eyebrow.

Randolph holds out his musket and laughs again. "No! No! I gave that rusty old blunderbuss to my nephew Joshua. Now this—!" And he shakes his weapon. "This is a *fine* instrument."

Of course! you think. Where are the turkey feathers?

Randolph invites you to spend the night at the settlement. Even though you're anxious to get back to your mission, you're rather tired and hungry, and you could use a good night's sleep.

The next day, refreshed and raring to go, you bid farewell to Randolph, his family, and the other settlers. So Josh might not have fired the first official shot of the war, but he still had the right musket. Even so, the flow of history somehow depends on a jump back in time to Fort William and Mary.

You walk until Randolph and his family are out of sight, and then jump!

Turn to page 55.

You arrive near the rebel general Charles Lee's headquarters near Monmouth, New Jersey, on the night of June 26, 1778. Although the sun has been down for several hours, the air is still very warm and humid. The ground remains waterlogged from the last rainfall.

The coming Battle of Monmouth will be fought under tropical conditions.

Over six thousand men are under Lee's command, and Joshua Shutesbury is somewhere among them. You can't begin to come up with an honest means of obtaining the rifle until you find him.

You hope he still has it.

You trudge into the perimeters of the camp, just a few miles away from the Monmouth courthouse. Half-expecting to be hailed by sentries at any moment, you finally notice that people of all sorts—mostly laborers and women—seem to come and go as they please.

Overhead the twinkling stars are unobscured by mountains, trees, or clouds. In fact the storm clouds are billowing at the borders of the horizon. Right now the camp is in the eye of the storm.

A few men discuss the constellations, and

especially the bright star you know to be Jupiter.

Other men merely clean their rifles and talk softly among themselves as they listen to the sounds of the British regiments and supplies moving in the distance. They seem bored and tense at the same time.

You walk up to a group of six men. "Excuse me, sirs, I was wondering if you could help me. I'm looking for someone."

"Who isn't?" the fat one laughs.

"What for?" asks the grizzled one.

"What's his name?" inquires a third, friendlier than the rest.

You decide it would be best if you answered the second question, but you're not sure what to say. "I've . . . uh . . . he's a friend of mine."

"Owes you money, huh?" says the grizzled one. "Forget it. Not a man in this camp has been paid a shilling in three months."

"And we won't get it until the French give it to us," says the fat one.

"Come looking for your friend after the war," chuckles a man drinking wine. As an officer rides by, he hides the bottle behind him, then gives it to the next man.

"What's his name?" insists the friendly one. "Or his regiment?"

"I don't know his regiment," you confess. "He's from Connecticut, I think. His name is Joshua Shutesbury."

Some of the men shake their heads. "Forget it," chuckles the friendly one, taking the wine. "We can't help you."

Well, that couldn't have gone any worse, you observe as you walk away. You know you can explore this entire camp if you must, but you also know you'll need a friend, and a place to fit into this society, if you're going to eat or have a place to sleep.

"You! Wait!" shouts someone running up behind you.

Assuming he obviously must be talking to someone else, you continue walking, searching for Joshua.

A young boy puts a hand on your shoulder, scaring you half out of your wits.

"Hey, our fife player's taken ill. We need another player," he says, holding up his own fife. "Interested in joining our regiment band?"

You have a fife! You've had it with you during your entire journey. Should you hook up with this person or not? Will it help you find Josh?

 Turn down the offer. Turn to page 92.

 Join the regiment band. Turn to page 81.

We owe you a hot meal for warning our families," says Randolph Shutesbury, as he and his friends walk toward the settlement.

You look at his musket. It could be the one that Randolph had at the Fort William and Mary incident that Joshua told you about, but right now there's no way to be sure.

"I've got a proposition for you," says Shutesbury a few minutes later. "You could probably use a few extra shillings, and we could use a few extra hands to do some work before the planting season starts. Why don't you stay on a few days and help out?"

You need to learn a little more about Randolph's musket, but doing farm work's going to take a lot of time from your mission.

You could take a good close look at the musket and jump to tonight when everybody's asleep. Maybe you can even take it.

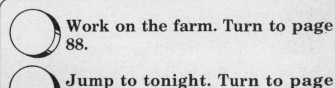

Work on the farm. Turn to page 88.

Jump to tonight. Turn to page 106.

ow march!" says the redcoat sergeant whose men have captured you and Lord Stirling during the Battle of Brooklyn.

You move to obey, but Stirling turns red, bristles, and spins about. "I may not be a genuine earl, sir, but I *am* an *officer of the enemy.* I demand to be treated with the respect due my station!"

The sergeant moves the bayonet on his musket closer to Stirling's face. "March, rebel!"

Stirling is unperturbed. His sole response is to put his hand on the hilt of his sword. "March where?" he asks after a tense moment.

"To the prisoner-of-war camp, of course!"

"Oh? Really?" asks Stirling. With a move quicker than lightning, he unsheathes the sword and presses the point against the sergeant's neck.

The other redcoats move forward, but Stirling halts them with an upraised palm. "Another step—and somebody will advance in the ranks." He grins slyly as the redcoats move back, then says to the sergeant, "I respectfully request an audience with General von Heister.

80

I shall surrender my sword to him personally!"

The sergeant slowly turns pale. Finally he nods and says, "Yes!"

Stirling nods with approval, but holds his sword in place. "Excellent. I knew I could make you see reason. Now I shall remove my threat to your person, but only after my friend here, who cannot possibly expect good treatment at your hands, has had ample opportunity to escape. Agreed?"

"Yes!" snarls the sergeant.

"Thanks, Lord Stirling," you say.

"Run, friend, run," he replies. "Run as if your life depends on it, for surely it does! Oh! And thank you, friend!"

His last words ring dimly in your ears, but you've already taken off. You reach a place in the marsh where the water is deep, look around, and see a couple of redcoats pointing their muskets in your direction.

You dive beneath the surface. Musket balls whisk by you like little torpedoes.

You've made some mistakes and you're still paying for them. There's only one thing to do—and that's to go back to where you made your first mistake. Return to the youth at Concord!

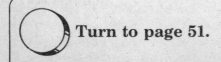

Turn to page 51.

ou're a fifer in the rebel forces during the Battle of Monmouth, but so far you haven't played any stirring songs.

General Charles Lee, the commander of the American forces, is showing a strange reluctance to engage his main forces in battle. Entire rebel troops are holding off the advancing redcoats, but instead of sending them support, Lee has ordered a general retreat. No one knows why. You hear the men grumbling among themselves. They're obviously discontent with Lee's decision. This was their chance to score a major victory against the enemy.

You've seen Lee twice, both times tending to the packs of dogs he owns. He takes them with him from camp to camp. He seems to care more about the dogs than he does for the soldiers.

The retreat is slow and hard. The supply wagons bog down in the mud, but the troops can't abandon them. The heat is unbelievable; the temperature must be over a hundred degrees.

You're frustrated because everything is too confused for you to try to find Josh. You're looking out for him, but everyone is too preoccupied with the dire situation to answer your questions. Not that you blame them. They sense the entire fate of the Revolution is at stake.

Around noon the retreat comes to a full stop. Men struggle in vain to get two artillery pieces past a muddy ravine. They use horses for pulling; they stand behind the cannon and push. But for all their efforts, the wheels sink deeper and deeper into the mud.

There is nothing for you to do but join the rest of the soldiers and sit beside the road.

Suddenly you notice a cloud of dust on the horizon. It rises up from the earth as if stirred by a great wind. The cloud can mean only one thing: the arrival of General Washington and his reinforcements!

An almost tangible excitement charges through the grimly silent men. The chance they've been waiting for is on the way!

General Lee, flanked by his staff officers and followed by his dogs, rides up. "Corporal, what is the reason for this delay?" he demands.

"The mud, sir!" impatiently replies a staff officer before the corporal can speak.

Revere tells them your name, adding, "My friend's been kind enough to assist me on a few occasions."

"Is that true?" Adams asks, looking you in the eye.

"Oh, yes, definitely," you say, still wondering why Revere pretends to know you so well.

In any case, Adams and Hancock both take you at your word and accept you as a fellow rebel. Jonas Clark makes you feel at home, and his wife serves you a slice of fresh-baked bread.

Adams and Hancock listen to Revere's report and conclude the area is unsafe for them. The redcoats may backtrack to the house, and they won't let a few white lies prevent them from searching it.

Adams and Hancock will go to nearby Wourn the first thing in the morning. Hancock will go with them.

All this is very interesting, but you realize none of it is helping you get to Lexington at the right time. You need an excuse to get out of here, one that will enable you to jump away without any of these influential people becoming suspicious of you.

The Reverend Clark yawns. "It's time we all got some sleep."

His wife gives you a blanket. "I'm afraid we haven't a place for you, but you'll be warm and comfortable in the barn."

Lee blinks at the officer, then at the ravine. "What? Oh, yes, I see. Well, bustle, men, bustle!"

Lee kicks his horse as if to ride farther up the line of retreat, but he halts almost immediately at the sight of a disheveled, red-haired Frenchman galloping toward the line.

"Lafayette! Your report!" snaps Lee with a haughty air.

"General Wayne's men are completely surrounded, sir," responds Lafayette. "I still don't know if they can get off the field. We must send them support!"

Lee bristles at the very thought. "Sir, you do not know British soldiers. We cannot stand long against them."

Everyone within hearing range is chilled to the marrow by the words. The Frenchman is about to reply when all are distracted by ragged but enthusiastic cheering at the head of the line.

Washington has arrived!

"Perhaps you would care to tell that to General Washington," says Lafayette as the general comes into view.

All the men come awake despite the stifling heat and their weariness. General Lee, in the meantime, awaits the confrontation with apparent stoicism.

General Washington rides up to Lee. "Sir! What is the meaning of this?" he demands.

His voice is trembling with repressed anger.

"Sir . . . Sir . . . !" Lee sputters indignantly.

Washington repeats the question.

"Well, sir, because of a variety of conflicting intelligence, and because my orders have not been obeyed, matters have been thrown into confusion. I chose not to risk the lives of my men under these circumstances. Besides, sir, if I may be so bold, an attack instead of a retreat is contrary to my own opinion."

Washington's face flushes. You notice that the scars on his cheeks, from an old smallpox attack, become particularly red. "Regardless of your opinion," he replies, "I gave you my orders, and I expect them to be obeyed."

"What, pray, are your orders *now*, sir?"

A grim silence falls between the men. The hubbub in the lines dies down to a whisper.

Finally General Washington says, "I order you off this field, *beyond* this field! You are to take no interest whatsoever in this battle. Is that understood, sir?"

Lee, who fought hard for this command, even when he thought he really didn't want it, practically fumes with rage. His face becomes as red as a British jacket.

Washington has been still and poised so far. Now he suddenly waves his palm violently in front of his face, as if to shoo away a fly. "And take your hounds with you!" he snaps. Lee is now as white as a ghost. "Yes, sir!" he says hoarsely, saluting.

Then Lee turns his horse and slinks away, taking his staff with him. Soon they are galloping across the field away from battle, followed by Lee's pack of barking dogs.

Without a trace of visible anger, Washington watches Lee go. That matter taken care of, he will now concentrate on the business at hand.

"How did things degenerate so?" he demands of the remaining officers. They look embarrassed. Even the trusted Lafayette seems reluctant to reply.

Then, without any warning whatsoever, Washington turns toward *you*! "Why don't you tell me?" Washington asks you.

"Ulp! Why me, sir?"

"I believe one who so forthrightly eavesdrops on a private conversation may have some opinions on it."

"You insist, sir?"

The general nods gravely.

"I think it has to do with, ah, bad communications. It must get pretty confusing with these officers talking via messengers when there's a fight going on. They may not even know when they're working at cross-purposes."

Washington leans back in the saddle and regards you severely. "Hah! The youth knows at least as much as I! Put down your fife—and become a messenger! We'll see if you're so critical of others after you've dodged musket balls!"

A messenger! Presumably you'll be sent from regiment to regiment, and as a result you'll have better chances of finding Shutesbury.

"Why, of course, sir!" you say cheerfully. "I love challenges!"

"Excellent. I can assign you to my staff or to that of the Marquis de Lafayette. Choose quickly! I've better things to do than haggle over messenger assignments."

He's right! Whom do you choose?

 John Washington's staff. Turn to page 100.

 Join Lafayette's staff. Turn to page 115.

ou help Randolph Shutesbury and the other settlers for three days, but learn nothing more about his musket. You don't know if he fired the first shot at the Fort William and Mary incident, or even if he still has the same musket.

This morning you've joined him on a hunting expedition, and so far the only thing you've learned is that keeping up with him is just as difficult as working on the farm.

Randolph practically scrambles up and down the hills and mountains, and it's all you can do to keep him in sight.

"Wait! Let's take a break!" you implore as the big man begins to clamber up a steep slope.

"Not now! And be quiet! These tracks are fresh!"

What tracks? you wonder, vainly looking for the signs Randolph sees in the trail as he climbs over some rocks.

Randolph moves up the slope like a buck-skinned wildcat. He soon reaches the top and moves out of sight. Everything is quiet for several minutes.

Suddenly the silence is shattered by the boom of his musket.

Something falls in the distance.

You scramble up the rest of the way to see Randolph already trotting toward a slain deer.

"Hurry!" he shouts. "There's fresh meat for supper tonight—and maybe a new pair of trousers for me!"

"That was quite a shot," you say after you've caught up.

"I confess, I impressed myself with that one. Never would have made it, though, without this musket. It's definitely an improvement over the one I shot that redcoat with at Fort William and Mary, back in my militia days."

"What happened to that one?" you ask, trying to sound casual, though your heart thunders in your ears.

Randolph kneels beside the deer. "Oh, I gave it to my nephew, Joshua."

Turkey feathers and all! you realize. You've spent the last few days on a wild-goose chase, but at least you now know the truth for certain. You *must* find Josh.

"Hey! Watch out!" cries Randolph, reaching toward you.

You've been backing up without realizing

it, and now you've inadvertently tripped over a ledge. You're falling down a ravine.

I hate falling, you think, just before you pass into the forest foliage. At least you're out of Randolph's sight, but you have approximately a tenth of a second to jump before you hit the ground.

Hurry, before the last sound you hear is *splat!*

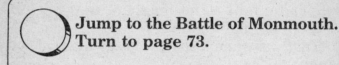

Jump to the Battle of Monmouth. Turn to page 73.

You've spent several hours wandering around the rebel camp the night before the Battle of Monmouth, looking for Joshua Shutesbury. So far you've had no luck whatsoever.

Someone behind you shouts, "Hey! You!"

Maybe it's the fifer giving you a second chance to join the military band. You turn around in anticipation.

But no! It's a teenaged girl! She's dressed in breeches and a man's shirt, and has an aristocratic air about her. "Who are you?" she asks. "What are you doing, wandering around here like a lost soul?"

"I, uh, live in Monmouth. I'm looking for, ah, my brother."

"So you live around here?" she asks.

"Well, not for long."

"Good enough," she says. "My name's Amanda Perry. My father is an officer under General Lee, and he has an urgent message that must get to General Washington, who's camped in Allentown. Things can get pretty dangerous in the countryside, with all the redcoat patrols, and I don't want to make the trip alone. Do you want to come with me?"

Hmmm. It's possible Joshua is actually at Allentown tonight. In any case, if you help her, you might meet someone who can help you find him.

Or you can forget this Battle of Monmouth business and jump to a place where it might be easier to find Josh—his fiancée's farm.

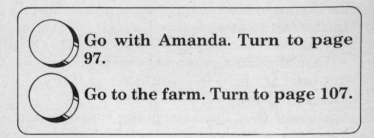

Go with Amanda. Turn to page 97.

Go to the farm. Turn to page 107.

You're standing at attention behind a troop of soldiers practicing drill at General Washington's winter camp in Valley Forge.

To make matters worse, you're face-to-face with Baron Friedrich Wilhelm Ludolf Gerhard Augustin von Steuben, the Prussian officer who helped turn Washington's ragtag army into crack troops during that harrowing winter.

Von Steuben, whose understanding of English is practically nonexistent, turns to his assistant and spews out a flurry of German phrases.

The assistant raises an eyebrow and smiles benignly at you. "The baron respectfully requests your name."

You tell him, quickly adding that you're a fife player. You hold out your fife as proof.

The assistant nods. He and von Steuben confer for several rapid sentences, and then the assistant again turns to you. "The baron says that since you appear so interested in how the troops are benefiting from his instruction, the least he can do is provide you with, ah, firsthand experience. *Fall in!*"

"No, really," you protest, "I just made a wrong turn. I don't need to march. Really!"

"FALL IN!" screams the baron in his thick Prussian accent.

"Yes, sir!" you reply, saluting enthusiastically.

Then you march. Judging from the position of the stark sun overhead, the time is about ten in the morning. This is not good. Von Steuben drilled his men until six at night.

You've eight hours to go. . . .

Eight hours you spend picking up some of the skills von Steuben introduced to the rebel army—skills that do nothing to help you find Joshua and his musket.

Night falls—finally! Von Steuben dismisses the troops, and then it's an easy matter for you to slip into the woods beyond the reach of prying eyes.

The temperature must be twenty below. You aren't dressed for this kind of weather.

Sitting on a log, you consider your options. You can go back to Monmouth to look for Joshua before the battle. Or you can go to the Pennsylvania frontier on the chance that his uncle Randolph still has the musket.

Better decide fast, before you turn into an iceberg!

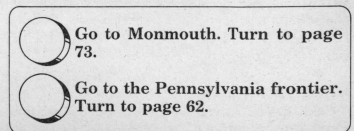

Go to Monmouth. Turn to page 73.

Go to the Pennsylvania frontier. Turn to page 62.

You're riding with Amanda Perry to give a message to General Washington in Allentown the night before the Battle of Monmouth. You hope to find Joshua Shutesbury, and the musket, among Washington's troops.

"There's another patrol!" says Amanda, pointing toward a redcoat squad marching across the field. "Quick, let's hide in this grove of trees," she adds, turning her horse.

You follow her. You haven't ridden very much, and your horse is very difficult to control. Fortunately, it follows Amanda's horse into a grove. The two of you wait silently as the redcoats go by.

Suddenly your horse neighs. The redcoat sergeant says, "In that grove of trees! That's where the rebels we spotted are!"

The redcoats rush toward the grove. You

and Amanda ride your horse to the back of the grove, only to find yourselves cut off by a brick wall too high to jump over.

"Listen, Amanda," you say, "I'll distract them. You take advantage of the opportunity to get away to Allentown."

"No! I can't let you face that danger alone!" she protests.

"Don't worry about me," you reply. "I can take care of myself. You just get that message to General Washington. Promise?" Before she can object again you ride straight toward the advancing redcoats.

They're so surprised by your bold move that they stand frozen. They begin scattering only when you're almost upon them.

Suddenly your horse stumbles in a gopher hole. It falls, and you fly out of the saddle. You hit the ground with a thud.

When you've recovered your senses, you see that the horse is galloping away, and the redcoats are rushing toward you.

You lead them on a wild chase through the field. They shoot at you, but you don't make a very good target in the night. Still, this is a dangerous game. You hope Amanda has had enough time to get away. After all, it was *your* horse who attracted the redcoats' attention in the first place.

Suddenly you see her on top of a hill, silhouetted in the moon. She disappears to the other side. The message will get through to General Washington!

You look around. Two redcoats, not twenty yards away, kneel to take shots at you. You're in open ground. If only you can make it to that clump of bushes . . . !

You dive just as the musket balls whizz by. You roll into the bushes. No one can see you for the moment. You've got to get out of this jam!

Jump!

 Turn to page 94.

You've become one of General Washington's messengers during the Battle of Monmouth. You'll move from company to company, and have a greater chance of finding Joshua Shutesbury.

Still you can't help but wonder if you should have gone back to the rear with Lafayette. It would have been much safer there.

You hang back from the actual fighting, awaiting a hand signal from General Washington that he needs you. Washington stays unusually close to the front lines for a general. He's always right on the spot, telling the soldiers exactly where he wants them to stand. He seems oblivious to the cannon fire and slaughter going on about him.

Finally he signals you to come. You run up as quickly as possible, dodging a few blasts along the way.

Washington calmly recites a few orders, which his assistant hastily scribbles on a piece of brown parchment. You stand and wait. This is hardly the time for small talk, though there are a million questions you want to ask Washington.

Suddenly, without warning, Washington's unflappable manner breaks. "What are you waiting for, chucklehead? Deliver that message! There's a war on here!" he barks.

"Yes, sir!"

Fortunately for you, Washington also points you in the proper direction. You run along the back of the lines, toward the artillery bank north of the rebel position. You keep your head low, to avoid stray musket balls.

You crawl up a small hill on your hands and knees. From the top you glimpse the New Englanders, placed at a fence, bearing the brunt of a redcoat offense. The rebels pull back, re-form their ranks, and turn upon the charging redcoats like seasoned professional soldiers.

In the distance, the British are changing the angle and position of their cannon. You sense that this means trouble.

Sure enough, before you're halfway down the other side of the hill, the cannon fire is smashing it into minced dirt. You suppose the British have decided that if they can't take the hill, no one else will get it either.

A few minutes later the rebel artillery bank is close at hand. You peer through the haze of dust and smoke for someone who looks as if he knows something—such as who is in charge here.

It doesn't seem as though anybody's in charge. The only officer's uniform you see is being worn by a dead body, lying beside a shattered tree. You wonder if it would have helped if he had received the message.

It's difficult to see through all the smoke. You look around for an officer, or even a familiar face.

Over there, beneath the branches of a chestnut tree, stands Joshua Shutesbury! He kneels, picks up a cannonball, and rolls it down the barrel. His legs wobble. He looks as if he's about to faint.

You're glad to see him, but where's his rifle?

The cannon recoils from the force of its explosion, and you glimpse the panache of turkey feathers. The musket is leaning against the chestnut tree!

You dash toward Joshua as the barrage of artillery fire escalates. It looks like a meteor shower!

Men duck and hide under what cover there is, but a large woman continues to load the cannon next to Josh's. Even through the din of battle you can hear her swear and holler in a husky voice.

Who is she? you wonder. You guess now's not the time to find out.

As you watch, a cannonball rips off part of her petticoat. She glances around for a second, then continues loading and firing the cannon.

The British score a direct hit on Josh's cannon. It explodes in pieces that fly high in the air, spraying the area with shrapnel. You dive to the ground.

When you look up, the woman is still helping the crew load the other cannon, and Josh's companions lie wounded or dead amid the debris.

But Josh is nowhere to be seen.

"Josh!" you call, racing toward where you last saw him. But he isn't there, and neither is his musket.

Then where is he?

Looking across the open field, where the New Englanders and redcoats are locked in mortal combat, you see Josh, musket in hand, staggering away from the action.

He's shell-shocked, you realize. You'll have to go after him.

And you do. "Josh! Josh!" you cry. "It's me, remember? We met at Concord!"

Behind you the woman with the loud voice shouts, "Wait, you bloody fool! What do you think you're doing?"

Josh stops, turns slightly, shakes his head, then finally sees you. He takes a step in your direction. Just as you're about to catch up with him, something explodes near you.

That's the last thing you remember before blacking out.

 Turn to page 108.

You're outside the Shutesbury house in the middle of the night. This was not a terrific idea, you think, sneaking around the house. Maybe you should just get out of here.

Wait! There's a musket outside on the porch. It's propped up under the window. Well, it won't hurt to take a look.

You creep onto the porch and reach for the musket. But before you touch it, you hear someone—or something—sniffling around the corner of the house.

You freeze. The sniffling grows louder.

You watch, transfixed, as a skinny dog sticks his snout around the cabin and goes *Yap! yap! yap! yap!*

"What's out there, Rover?" calls a voice from inside. You take off. The dog takes off after you. He nips at your heels, but you can't worry about that now. You've got to get out of firing range.

No time to think! Jump!

Turn to page 39.

You're on the Connecticut farm where Joshua Shutesbury's fiancée lives. With luck, Josh may be here, or may be visiting soon.

You hear some noises in the barn. You knock and peek in. "Hello? Anybody home?"

A girl of about sixteen is milking a cow. "Who are you?" she asks.

You tell her. "I'm looking for Joshua," you add.

"So am I," she says, smiling and shaking your hand. "My name's Judith Harman. Josh and I got engaged before all the shooting started at Lexington and Concord, but I haven't laid eyes on him since."

"Oh? Do you know where he might be?"

"Of course. He writes me all the time. He can't spell well, but the meaning's always clear. He's under General Lee's command."

Which means you've sent yourself on a wild-goose chase! Joshua was at Monmouth all along! You thank Judith and leave.

Jump to Monmouth.
Turn to page 73.

You awaken in a haze of pain. The last thing you remember was being thrown into the air by an explosion.

Now you're lying on the ground in a makeshift tent, among the wounded and dying soldiers, after the Battle of Monmouth. Your bedding consists only of a smelly blanket. Someone's ragged coat is your pillow.

A large woman carries a bucket of water from man to man, permitting each a single drink from a wooden spoon.

You recognize her from the battlefield. She was the woman loading the cannon. Now you remember who she is.

"You're Molly Pitcher!" you say when she reaches you.

"That's what I hear," she says, kneeling beside you. "Though how you figured it out in your sleep, I'll never know."

You smile weakly. "A lucky guess."

"Humph." She gives you a spoonful of water. The warm liquid tastes bitter. She says, "And I know who you are: someone who's lucky to be alive. I saw you chasing after that boy on the battlefield."

Returning the spoon, you explain that he was a friend.

"He must be a good friend indeed," she says, "for you to take an awful risk like that."

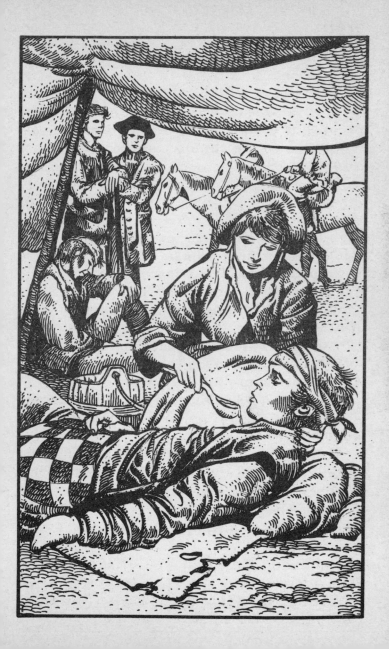

110

"What do you think might have happened to him?"

She shrugs. "It's hard to say. From the direction he was headed, I'd judge he was picked up either by the redcoats or by Hessian deserters. They're rumored to be somewhere around here."

Hessians! Those were the German mercenaries hired by the British to help them fight the colonists!

"Molly . . . Molly . . ." croaks the soldier beside you, a man whose arm and face are wrapped in bloody bandages.

"I'm needed somewhere else, youngster," Molly says, turning around. "Hope you find your friend."

You're very lucky. You feel a little stiff, but otherwise you're none the worse for wear. A few bruises are your only injuries.

Soon the other soldiers in the makeshift tent fall asleep. You'll be able to jump without anybody seeing you.

But where to? To find British soldiers who might have captured Josh? Or to find the Hessian deserters?

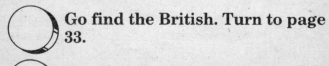

Go find the British. Turn to page 33.

Go find the Hessians. Turn to page 116.

In a few hours it will be dawn. The redcoats are sound asleep—at least, you hope they are.

"Sssh!" you whisper to Josh as you cut his ropes with the Swiss army knife. "Don't make a move."

"Who—?" he asks.

"Quiet! You'll wake them!"

As if to prove your point, the rotund redcoat grumbles and turns in his sleep. He was the last one to pass out. And it took him quite a while.

"I remember you!" Josh exclaims, rubbing his wrists to restore circulation.

Meanwhile, you cut loose his feet. "Quiet! We can reminisce later. Where's your musket?"

"Right there," replies Josh, pointing to where it lies, beside the tall redcoat—who's passed out with his feet practically in the dying embers. Josh stands to get the musket, staggers, and leans on you for support.

When he can stand by himself—though he's still wobbly—you say, "I'll get it." You move softly—ever so softly—toward the sleeping redcoat. Just as you near him, he laughs and reaches out toward you. You freeze. He's got you for sure, you think. But then he giggles and rolls over.

He's dreaming! you realize, picking up the musket without making a sound.

You and Josh slip into the relative safety of the New Jersey forest.

 Turn to page 120.

ust after you become
Lafayette's messenger, General Washington
takes him aside and orders him to the rear
lines.

"The situation is dire," Washington says.
"We must regroup—quickly—before the attack is upon us. If we must retreat—well, I'd
prefer to know that one of my most dependable
officers is commanding the troops guarding
my backside."

"Very well," says Lafayette, his disappoint-
ment plain. "Come, my friend," says the
Frenchman, leaning over and reaching out his
hand. He pulls you up behind him.

You ride with him as he leads his troops to
the rear, where they rest and wait beneath
the merciless sun.

Unfortunately, Josh is not among them.

Since you can't jump back to join Washington's staff—the rebels are bound to think
something's up if there are suddenly two of
you—you decide to jump back a few hours, to
last night at the camp. Perhaps there you'll
find another route to Josh.

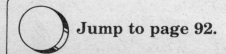 **Jump to page 92.**

ou are twenty yards from the Hessian camp. You don't see Josh anywhere among them—but as you look for him, the Hessian deserters are looking at you!

You start running a few seconds before they take off after you. The moon is full and bright, which means they can see you quite clearly in the field. You can't jump anywhere without being seen—not yet, anyway.

Judging from the sound of their laughter, the Hessians are catching up with you fast. There's no telling what they'll do when they catch you.

But you can guess at what might distract them, giving you a chance to get away.

"Here, do you want this?" you call out, holding out your fife. You turn around just long enough to see if they're interested.

They are. You throw away the fife. As you continue running, you hear two of the Hessians fighting over it. Each claims to be the better player.

"How about this?" you call out, holding another item. "And *this?* And *this?*"

In a few moments you've thrown away everything you brought with you. You're down to nothing but your clothes.

A quick glance behind you reveals that your tactic has worked. The men who had been chasing you are now scrounging in the field for goodies. They're paying absolutely no attention to you!

Now's your chance to see if Josh has been captured by the British.

 Turn to page 33.

ou smear dirt all over your face. You figure that this will make it harder for the drowsy redcoats to see you approach.

The sun has been in the sky for about an hour, but the air is still pretty cold. Both Josh and the redcoats have been asleep for some time. From your vantage point, Josh is concealed behind a log. Occasionally you hear him tossing about, kicking his legs against the ground. Maybe he's having a bad dream.

Now's as good a time as any to put your plan into action. You run at top speed toward the camp. Your whole mission is at stake!

You scream at the top of your lungs. With luck, you should catch them sufficiently off-guard so you and Josh can fight your way out of camp.

You leap into the air and land on the rotund redcoat's ample tummy. He was just beginning to realize something was up. The breath goes out of him like the air from a deflating tire. Hoping to jump from him directly onto the tall redcoat, you bend your knees and prepare to make your move.

Unfortunately, the rotund redcoat is not so disabled that he can't trip you in mid-jump.

You hit the ground. Hard.

The three redcoats are on top of you before you can even begin to get up. They tie you up like a chicken in a truss.

"Thought you would scare us out of our wits, did you?" sneers the rotund one at you.

"There!" says the tall one, slapping his hands in grim satisfaction when the job is done. "Now we have *two* rebel prisoners."

"Uh, I don't know how to tell you this," says the short redcoat meekly, "but we still only have *one* prisoner."

"Eh?"

"What?"

The short one just points.

You look with them to the place where Josh used to be. He and his musket are gone; all that's left behind are his severed bonds and the sharp rock he cut them with.

Josh wasn't sleeping at all! He was engineering his own escape and took advantage of the confusion to escape by himself.

That's great for him. But what about you?

 Turn to page 60.

Y

ou and Josh are several hundred yards away before he remembers where he's seen you before. "I met you at Concord!" he says.

You smile. "You sure did. I was hoping I'd run into you again."

"How did you know where to find me?" he asks.

After reciting a slightly revised version of the facts, you add good-naturedly, "Actually, I wasn't interested in you so much as I was in your musket."

Josh laughs. "Well, it's a fine piece of hardware, as they say. It's almost an antique, though."

"Don't you have a sentimental attachment to it?"

"Why should I?" Josh asks in all seriousness.

You've just assumed he'd want to keep it as much as you want it. "Well, it does belong in your family," you say.

"That it does. But I've an even greater sentimental attachment to my life. I need a musket I can depend on, and pretty soon this one isn't going to be it."

The two of you decide to take a break. You

sit on the riverbank, watching the rapids foaming over the rocks.

"Wonder how the fishing is today," you muse aloud, prompted by a sudden hunger pain in your stomach.

"We don't have time to find out," Josh replies. "I've got to return to my company. I— Quiet! Listen!"

You do as he says. Three seconds later, Josh stands, grabs his musket by the barrel, and breaks it across the chest of the rotund redcoat who was sneaking up behind you.

You don't know which development horrifies you the most: that the musket you came for is broken in two . . . or that without warning, you and Josh are suddenly being held at bayonet point by the other redcoats.

Well, at least one of the three is out of commission.

You raise your hands. Still holding onto the pieces of the musket, Josh does likewise.

"Now there's not going to be any more trouble from you two, is there?" says the tall redcoat.

"You're coming with us," says the short one. "And then you'll most likely go to the *Jersey*."

"A fate you well deserve. Keep them both covered!" the tall redcoat says as he lowers his musket and advances forward. "I like those turkey feathers," he says, holding out his free hand. "Give them to me."

"Gladly," says Josh, smiling, just before he smashes the butt across the redcoat's face.

The wood makes a sickening crack. The redcoat begins to slump to the ground. Josh drops what's left of his musket and catches him, using him as a shield against the other man.

Then it's Josh who advances forward, carrying his enemy with every step.

The short redcoat is no less amazed than you at this unexpected turn. His face begins to sweat, his knees quiver, and the point of his bayonet shakes. "Go ahead," taunts Josh, "but your buddy's going to go first!"

The redcoat screams in anger and frustration, drops his musket, and hightails it into the forest.

Josh lets the tall redcoat fall to the ground, then laughs long and hard. "Well, that was certainly a restful spell," he says when he can control himself.

You finally permit yourself a sigh of relief. "It was definitely a close call."

Josh looks at you quizzically until he figures out the meaning of your expression. "I don't think so. Those redcoats were cowardly, not like the usual sort. Otherwise they'd have rejoined their unit and taken their medicine, rather than going through all that effort just to look good."

"But because of them, you broke your musket."

Josh shrugs nonchalantly. "It was just a piece of hardware, built for a purpose. And it served it." He looks down at you and smiles. "But I notice you had a fondness for it."

"Can I take it?" you ask, trying to restrain your eagerness. "Maybe I can get it fixed somehow."

"Sure. Why not?"

You and Josh part ways before the fallen redcoats come to. He's going back to the rebel army to continue the fight for independence, and you can return to your time.

Like the Liberty Bell, the musket that fired the first shot of the revolutionary war did not survive its service intact.

Your mission is complete. But more important than your mission, you've learned that the revolutionary war was fought by people, good, bad, and indifferent, not unlike the people of your time—men and women brave enough to stand by their freedom in the best way they knew how.

History doesn't say what happened to Joshua Shutesbury. You hope, for his sake, that his fight proved to be worthwhile.

MISSION COMPLETED.

DATA FILE

About the Contributors

ARTHUR BYRON COVER is a novelist, comic-book scripter, editor, writing teacher, and professional bookseller in Los Angeles. He is author of *Autumn Angels* and *An Eastwind Coming* and is currently at work on his third Time Machine book.

WALTER P. MARTISHIUS is a book illustrator and theatrical set designer. He has done illustrations for the computer games *Dragonworld* and *Starman Jones*. He is presently getting a master's degree in motion picture set design from the University of Massachusetts. He lives in Holland, Ohio.

ALEX NINO is an internationally respected illustrator. His work has appeared in such publications as *Metal Hurlant* in France, *Starlog* in America, and hundreds of magazines in his native Philippines. For the Time Machine series he is the illustrator of *Search for Dinosaurs* and *Civil War Secret Agent,* and co-illustrator of *Sail with Pirates.* He is also the winner of an Inkpot Award.

BLAST INTO THE PAST!

TIME MACHINE

Each of these books is a time machine and you are at the controls . . .

- [ ] 23601 **SECRETS OF THE KNIGHTS #1** $1.95
  J. Gasperini
- [ ] 25399 **SEARCH FOR DINOSAURS #2** $2.25
  D. Bischoff
- [ ] 25619 **SWORD OF THE SAMURAI #3** $2.25
  M. Reaves & S. Perry
- [ ] 25616 **SAIL WITH PIRATES #4** $2.25
  J. Gasperini
- [ ] 25606 **CIVIL WAR SECRET AGENT #5** $2.25
  Steve Perry
- [ ] 24424 **THE RINGS OF SATURN #6** $1.95
  Arthur Cover
- [ ] 24722 **ICE AGE EXPLORER #7** $1.95
  Dougal Dixon
- [ ] 25073 **THE MYSTERY OF ATLANTIS #8** $2.25
  Jim Gasperini
- [ ] 25180 **WILD WEST RIDER #9** $2.25
  Stephen Overholser

Prices and availability subject to change without notice.

Buy them at your local bookstore or use this handy coupon for ordering:

Bantam Books, Inc., Dept. TM, 414 East Golf Road, Des Plaines, Ill. 60016

Please send me the books I have checked above. I am enclosing $_____
(please add $1.25 to cover postage and handling. Send check or money
order—no cash or C.O.D.'s please).

Mr/Ms _____

Address _____

City/State _____ Zip _____

TM—11/85

Please allow four to six weeks for delivery. This offer expires 5/86.